Grumpy Bear

Best Friend Bear

Secret Bear

This book belongs to:
TAYLOR RB

Wish Bear

Love-a-lot Bear

Published by Scholastic Inc.
90 Old Sherman Turnpike, Danbury, CT 06816.

SCHOLASTIC and associated logos are trademarks and/or registered trademarks of Scholastic Inc.

ISBN 0-439-84303-0

First Scholastic Printing, July 2006

Care Bears™ Friendship Club

One Friend at a Time

by
Quinlan B. Lee

Illustrated by
Saxton Moore

SCHOLASTIC INC.

New York   Toronto   London   Auckland   Sydney
Mexico City   New Delhi   Hong Kong   Buenos Aires

It was another sunny day in Care-a-lot.

"I love playing kickball!" Funshine Bear exclaimed.

"It always reminds me of the first day I came to Care-a-lot."

"I remember that," said Cheer Bear. "You had a rainbow ball, and you taught us all how to play. That was so fun!"

"Everything is fun in Care-a-lot," said Love-a-lot Bear.
"When I first came here,

I loved it right away."

"And there are so many friends to share in the fun,"
Share Bear said. "Care-a-lot is the best place in the world."

Bashful Heart Bear smiled timidly. "When I first came to Care-a-lot, I didn't like it very much," he said quietly. "It took me a long time to share in the fun."

"Why?" asked Share Bear.
"There's always plenty of fun for everyone."

"Oh, I know that now," said Bashful Heart Bear. "But new places can be scary—especially for a shy bear like me."

Funshine Bear shrugged and asked, "Why were you shy? We're tons of fun."

"And we're easy to love," Love-a-lot Bear chimed in.

Bashful Heart Bear nodded. "That's true," he said. "But it wasn't easy getting to know all of the Care Bears. There were so many of you, and just one of me."

"So what happened?" asked Cheer Bear.

"Well, the first thing that happened was Share Bear invited me to one of her parties. I really wanted to come, but I felt a little bashful because I didn't know anyone's name. So I decided just to play by myself instead," Bashful Heart Bear said.

"Then the next day, Funshine Bear came and asked me to go roller skating. Funshine Bear was so friendly that I decided to go," said Bashful Heart Bear.

"While I was putting on my skates, Funshine Bear began a skate train," Bashful Heart Bear added. "Skate trains are the best!" said Best Friend Bear. "Did you have fun?"

"Not really," Bashful Heart Bear replied. "All that chasing and racing kind of scared me. So I decided to go pick flowers instead."

"So then how *did* you get to know us?" wondered Cheer Bear.

Secret Bear smiled. "It's no secret to me how I got to know Bashful Heart Bear. He went to pick flowers in *my* secret flower patch."

"That's right!" said Bashful Heart Bear. "You sat down beside me, quiet as a secret, and started picking flowers, too."

Secret Bear agreed. "After a while, we started talking."

"The next day, Secret Bear invited me to go stargazing with her," Bashful Heart Bear said.

"I was still a little shy, but I really liked Secret Bear, so I decided to go."

Bashful Heart Bear continued, "Then when Secret Bear and I were stargazing . . ."

"...you met me!" said Wish Bear. "I remember that!"

"That's right!" Bashful Heart Bear said.
"And I made a wish that I would make even
more friends."

"And you know me," said Wish Bear. "A wish made is a wish made true. So a little while later Share Bear came by with hot chocolate, and..."

"... I became your friend!" Share Bear added.

Bashful Heart Bear said, "Then later, Bedtime Bear came to tuck us all in. By the time I fell asleep, I had four new friends in Care-a-lot."

29

Bashful Heart Bear looked around at all the
Care Bears, and said, "One by one I got to know

each of you, and then I didn't
feel shy anymore."

"I think I understand now," said Funshine Bear.
"So we can be shy and still love to have lots of fun."

"Or lots of friends?" Love-a-lot Bear asked.

"Right," said Bashful Heart Bear. "Being shy just means you're best at picking your friends one at a time."

"Is that like picking flowers?" asked Best Friend Bear.

Bashful Heart Bear laughed. "It sure is!" he said.
"And I just kept picking one by one, until I had. . .

the biggest and best
bouquet of friends ever!"

Do you sometimes feel shy like Bashful Heart Bear?

Bashful Heart Bear felt shy the first time he came to Care-a-lot.

♥ Does being in a new place make you feel shy?

♥ How can you feel less bashful in a new place?

Secret Bear was Bashful Heart Bear's first friend in Care-a-lot. What did she do to make him feel better?

♥ Do you know people who are shy that you could get to know?

♥ What could you do to become their friend?

It was easier for Bashful Heart Bear to make friends one at a time.

♥ How about you?

♥ Which do you like better: playing with lots of friends or playing with one special friend?

Bashful Heart Bear

Cheer Bear

Share Bear

Bedtime Bear

Funshine Bear